At the Market

D1494764

Graeme Beals

PINNACLE PRESS

At the Market is the second in a five book series.
Tom and Tammy have a fun day at the market,
but then Tammy's attention is drawn away by
another guy - a big guy!.

Titles follow in this sequence:

Tom and Tammy – At the Market
ISBN 9781906125998
Ordering Code – UK7000

Curriculum Concepts UK
The Old School
Upper High Street
Bedlinog
Mid-Glamorgan CF46 6SA

Email: orders@curriculumconcepts.co.uk
www.curriculumconcepts.co.uk

Illustrated by Ross Bennett

Tammy and I go into the market.

Many people are there.

We look at the stalls.

We see some pictures.

We touch some soft toys.

Tammy smells some strong cheese.

I taste some bread.

Tammy buys a candle.

I think she is nice!

We come to the clothes.

There are clothes for girls and guys.

Clothes of every colour.

There are tops of all shapes.

There are pants of every size.

Tammy and I laugh.

Tammy tries on a skirt.

She comes and shows me.

"I like it," I say.

Tammy buys it because I liked it.

I feel good.

I look at some jeans.

I try some on.

"They look cool," says Tammy.

I buy them because she likes them.

It is time to go.

We are leaving the market.

Tammy sees another guy.

He says, "Hi Tammy," to her.

Tammy stops to talk to him.

He is big.

I feel small and angry.

I walk away.